CAROL DIGGORY SHIELDS

illustrated by PAUL MEISEL

I WISH MY BROTHER WAS A DOG

PUFFIN BOOKS

PUFFIN BOOKS
Published by the Penguin Group
Penguin Putnam Books for Young Readers, 345 Hudson Street, New York, NY 10014, U.S.A.
Penguin Books Ltd, 27 Wrights Lane, London W8 5TZ, England
Penguin Books Australia Ltd, Ringwood, Victoria, Australia
Penguin Books Canada Ltd, 10 Alcorn Avenue, Toronto, Ontario, Canada M4V 3B2
Penguin Books (N.Z.) Ltd, 182-190 Wairau Road, Auckland 10, New Zealand

Penguin Books Ltd, Registered Offices: Harmondsworth, Middlesex, England

First published in the United States of America by Dutton Children's Books, a division of Penguin Books USA Inc., 1997
Published by Puffin Books, a member of Penguin Putnam Books for Young Readers, 1999

3 5 7 9 10 8 6 4 2

Text copyright © Carol Diggory Shields, 1997. Illustrations copyright © Paul Meisel, 1997
THE LIBRARY OF CONGRESS HAS CATALOGED THE DUTTON EDITION AS FOLLOWS:
Shields, Carol Diggory.
I wish my brother was a dog / by Carol Diggory Shields; illustrated by Paul Meisel. 1st ed.   p.   cm.
Summary: An older sibling imagines how much better it would be if brother Andy were a dog
instead of a baby, doing tricks and being banished to the outside when he got too noisy.
ISBN 0-525-45464-0 (hc.)
[1. Babies—Fiction. 2. Dogs—Fiction.] I. Meisel, Paul, ill. II. Title.
PZ7.S554776Iae 1997 [E]—dc21 96-52712 CIP AC

Puffin Books ISBN 0-14-056191-9

Printed in the United States of America

For David and Sally, with love —C.D.S.

For my brothers, Jim, Gary, and Ron,
and for the real dog, Taffy —P.M.

I wish my brother was a dog!

Andy, I'd like you a lot better if you were a dog.

If you were a dog, I'd buy you some dog toys with my allowance. A chewy bone and lots of bouncy balls. You could play with them all the time and never, never, *never* touch my toys again.

Andy, you'd have a lot more hair if you were a dog. And a lot more teeth, too. Then you could be a watchdog! You could stay home and guard the house when Mom and I go out. All by ourselves. See you later, Andy!

Andy, if you were a dog, you wouldn't always be
smushing your peas and squishing your applesauce
and making a big mess at the table. You'd get to eat
out of a nice red bowl with your name on it, on the
kitchen floor. Andy's a good name for a dog.

Tricks, Andy! Dogs can do tricks! I could teach
you to shake hands and beg and jump through a hoop.
And we could play games like fetch and tug-of-war
and Frisbee.

We wouldn't have to listen to you cry anymore. If you were a dog, you could bark instead. And if you got too loud, we'd put you outside on the back steps.

You wouldn't have to sleep in my room in that squeaky old crib anymore, either. If you were a dog, you could sleep in the hall. Or we could build you a little house, just the right size—way, way out in the backyard.

Just think, Andy, if you were a dog, no more stinky diapers.

You could play out in the yard all afternoon if you were a dog. Dig holes and chase squirrels and roll in the mud. You wouldn't need a bath. We'd wash you off with a hose.

If you didn't feel good, we wouldn't fuss and worry
and carry you around and say, "Poor little baby-waby."
We'd take you to a vet, and he'd give you a shot.

And if Mom and Dad and I went somewhere, you wouldn't need to ride in your car seat in the back with me or stay at home with a grumpy baby-sitter. You could stay in a kennel.

If you were a dog, Andy, we could put you on a leash and take you to a dog show. You'd be the best dog there. You could show off all the tricks I taught you, and you might win a prize, Andy!

And then somebody might want to buy you!

Good-bye, Andy.

It would be real peaceful around here. No babies, no noise, no messed-up toys.

Maybe too peaceful.

You know what, Andy? Maybe I'll just keep you, if Mom says it's okay. I'd take real good care of you. Because if you were my dog, Andy, I'd treat you like you were…

my very own brother.